Elia W. Peattie

The Shape of Fear

and other Ghostly Tales

Elia W. Peattie

The Shape of Fear

and other Ghostly Tales

ISBN/EAN: 9783955630218

Auflage: 1

Erscheinungsjahr: 2013

Erscheinungsort: Bremen, Deutschland

Leseklassiker

CONTENTS

THE SHAPE OF FEAR

TIM O'CONNOR — who was descended from the O'Conors with one N — — started life as a poet and an enthusiast. His mother had designed him for the priesthood, and at the age of fifteen, most of his verses had an ecclesiastical tinge, but, somehow or other, he got into the newspaper business instead, and became a pessimistic gentleman, with a literary style of great beauty and an income of modest proportions. He fell in with men who talked of art for art's sake, — though what right they had to speak of art at all nobody knew, — and little by little his view of life and love became more or less profane. He met a woman who sucked his heart's blood, and he knew it and made no protest; nay, to the great amusement of the fellows who talked of art for art's sake, he went the length of marrying her. He could not in decency explain that he had the traditions of fine gentlemen behind him and so had to do as he did, because his friends might not have understood. He laughed at the days when he had thought of the priesthood, blushed when he ran across any of those tender and exquisite old verses he had written in his youth, and became addicted to absinthe and other less peculiar drinks, and to gaming a little to escape a madness of ennui.

As the years went by he avoided, with more and more scorn, that part of the world which he denominated Philistine, and consorted only with the fellows who flocked about Jim O'Malley's saloon. He was pleased with solitude, or with these convivial wits, and with not very much else beside. Jim O'Mal-

1

ley was a sort of Irish poem, set to inspiring measure. He was, in fact, a Hibernian Mæcenas, who knew better than to put bad whiskey before a man of talent, or tell a trite tale in the presence of a wit. The recountal of his disquisitions on politics and other current matters had enabled no less than three men to acquire national reputations; and a number of wretches, having gone the way of men who talk of art for art's sake, and dying in foreign lands, or hospitals, or asylums, having no one else to be homesick for, had been homesick for Jim O'Malley, and wept for the sound of his voice and the grasp of his hearty hand.

When Tim O'Connor turned his back upon most of the things he was born to and took up with the life which he consistently lived till the unspeakable end, he was unable to get rid of certain peculiarities. For example, in spite of all his debauchery, he continued to look like the Beloved Apostle. Notwithstanding abject friendships he wrote limpid and noble English. Purity seemed to dog his heels, no matter how violently he attempted to escape from her. He was never so drunk that he was not an exquisite, and even his creditors, who had become inured to his deceptions, confessed it was a privilege to meet so perfect a gentleman. The creature who held him in bondage, body and soul, actually came to love him for his gentleness, and for some quality which baffled her, and made her ache with a strange longing which she could not define. Not that she ever defined anything, poor little beast! She had skin the color of pale gold, and yellow eyes with brown lights in them, and great plaits of straw-colored hair.

About her lips was a fatal and sensuous smile, which, when it got hold of a man's imagination, would not let it go, but held to it, and mocked it till the day of his death. She was the incarnation of the Eternal Feminine, with all the wifeliness and the maternity left out — she was ancient, yet ever young, and familiar as joy or tears or sin.

She took good care of Tim in some ways: fed him well, nursed him back to reason after a period of hard drinking, saw that he put on overshoes when the walks were wet, and looked after his money. She even prized his brain, for she discovered that it was a delicate little machine which produced gold. By association with him and his friends, she learned that a number of apparently useless things had value in the eyes of certain convenient fools, and so she treasured the autographs of distinguished persons who wrote to him — autographs which he disdainfully tossed in the waste basket. She was careful with presentation copies from authors, and she went the length of urging Tim to write a book himself. But at that he balked.

"Write a book!" he cried to her, his gentle face suddenly white with passion. "Who am I to commit such a profanation?"

She didn't know what he meant, but she had a theory that it was dangerous to excite him, and so she sat up till midnight to cook a chop for him when he came home that night.

He preferred to have her sitting up for him, and he wanted every electric light in their apartments turned to the full. If, by any chance, they returned together to a dark house, he would not enter till she touched the button in the hall, and illuminated the room. Or if it so happened that the lights were turned off in the night time, and he awoke to find himself in darkness, he shrieked till the woman came running to his relief, and, with derisive laughter, turned them on again. But when she found that after these frights he lay trembling and white in his bed, she began to be alarmed for the clever, gold-making little machine, and to renew her assiduities, and to horde more tenaciously than ever, those valuable curios on which she some day expected to realize when he was out of the way, and no longer in a position to object to their barter.

O'Connor's idiosyncrasy of fear was a source of much amusement among the boys at the office where he worked. They made open sport of it, and yet, recognizing him for a sensitive plant, and granting that genius was entitled to whimsicalities, it was their custom when they called for him after work hours, to permit him to reach the lighted corridor before they turned out the gas over his desk. This, they reasoned, was but a slight service to perform for the most enchanting beggar in the world.

"Dear fellow," said Rick Dodson, who loved him, "is it the Devil you expect to see? And if so, why are you averse? Surely the Devil is not such a bad old chap."

"You haven't found him so?"

"Tim, by heaven, you know, you ought to explain to me. A citizen of the world and a student of its purlieus, like myself, ought to know what there is

4

to know! Now you're a man of sense, in spite of a few bad habits — such as myself, for example. Is this fad of yours madness? — which would be quite to your credit, — for gadzooks, I like a lunatic! Or is it the complaint of a man who has gathered too much data on the subject of Old Rye? Or is it, as I suspect, something more occult, and therefore more interesting?"

"Rick, boy," said Tim, "you're too — inquiring!" And he turned to his desk with a look of delicate hauteur.

It was the very next night that these two tippling pessimists spent together talking about certain disgruntled but immortal gentlemen, who, having said their say and made the world quite uncomfortable, had now journeyed on to inquire into the nothingness which they postulated. The dawn was breaking in the muggy east; the bottles were empty, the cigars burnt out. Tim turned toward his friend with a sharp breaking of sociable silence.

"Rick," he said, "do you know that Fear has a Shape?"

"And so has my nose!"

"You asked me the other night what I feared. Holy father, I make my confession to you. What I fear is Fear."

"That's because you've drunk too much — or not enough.

"'Come, fill the cup, and in the fire of Spring
Your winter garment of repentance fling — '"

"My costume then would be too nebulous for this weather, dear boy. But it's true what I was saying. I am afraid of ghosts."

"For an agnostic that seems a bit — "

"Agnostic! Yes, so completely an agnostic that I do not even know that I do not know! God, man, do you mean you have no ghosts — no — no things which shape themselves? Why, there are things I have done — "

"Don't think of them, my boy! See, 'night's candles are burnt out, and jocund day stands tiptoe on the misty mountain top.'"

Tim looked about him with a sickly smile. He looked behind him and there was nothing there; stared at the blank window, where the smoky dawn showed its offensive face, and there was nothing there. He pushed away the moist hair from his haggard face — that face which would look like the blessed St. John, and leaned heavily back in his chair.

"'Yon light is not daylight, I know it, I,'" he murmured drowsily, "'it is some meteor which the sun exhales, to be to thee this night — '"

The words floated off in languid nothingness, and he slept. Dodson arose preparatory to stretching himself on his couch. But first he bent over his friend with a sense of tragic appreciation.

"Damned by the skin of his teeth!" he muttered. "A little more, and he would have gone right, and the Devil would have lost a good fellow. As it is" — he smiled with his usual conceited delight in his own sayings, even when they were uttered in soliloquy — "he is merely one of those splendid gentlemen one will meet with in hell." Then Dodson had a momentary nostalgia for goodness himself, but he soon overcame it, and stretching himself on his sofa, he, too, slept.

That night he and O'Connor went together to hear "Faust" sung, and returning to the office, Dodson prepared to write his criticism. Except for the distant clatter of telegraph instruments, or the peremptory cries of "copy" from an upper room, the office was still. Dodson wrote and smoked his interminable cigarettes; O' Connor rested his head in his hands on the desk, and sat in perfect silence. He did not know when Dodson finished, or when, arising, and absent-mindedly extinguishing the lights, he moved to the door with his copy in his hands. Dodson gathered up the hats and coats as he passed them where they lay on a chair, and called:

"It is done, Tim. Come, let's get out of this."

There was no answer, and he thought Tim was following, but after he had handed his criticism to the city editor, he saw he was still alone, and returned to the room for his friend. He advanced no further than the doorway, for, as he stood in the dusky corridor and looked within the darkened room, he saw before his friend a Shape, white, of perfect loveliness, divinely delicate and pure and ethereal, which seemed as the embodiment of all goodness. From it came a soft radiance and a perfume softer than the wind when "it breathes upon a bank of violets stealing and giving odor." Staring at it, with eyes immovable, sat his friend.

It was strange that at sight of a thing so unspeakably fair, a coldness like that which comes from the jewel-blue lips of a Muir crevasse should have fallen upon Dodson, or that it was only by summoning all the manhood that was left in him, that he was able to restore light to the room, and to rush to his friend. When he reached poor Tim he was stone-still with paralysis. They took him home to the woman, who nursed him out of that attack — and later on worried him into another.

When he was able to sit up and jeer at things a little again, and help himself to the quail the woman broiled for him, Dodson, sitting beside him, said:

"Did you call that little exhibition of yours legerdemain, Tim, you sweep? Or are you really the Devil's bairn?"

"It was the Shape of Fear," said Tim, quite seriously.

"But it seemed mild as mother's milk."

"It was compounded of the good I might have done. It is that which I fear."

He would explain no more. Later — many months later — he died patiently and sweetly in the madhouse, praying for rest. The little beast with the yellow eyes had high mass celebrated for him, which, all things considered, was almost as pathetic as it was amusing.

Dodson was in Vienna when he heard of it.

"Sa, sa!" cried he. "I wish it wasn't so dark in the tomb! What do you suppose Tim is looking at?"

As for Jim O'Malley, he was with difficulty kept from illuminating the grave with electricity.

ON THE NORTHERN ICE

THE winter nights up at Sault Ste. Marie are as white and luminous as the Milky Way. The silence which rests upon the solitude appears to be white also. Even sound has been included in Nature's arrestment, for, indeed, save the still white frost, all things seem to be obliterated. The stars have a poignant brightness, but they belong to heaven and not to earth, and between their immeasurable height and the still ice rolls the ebon ether in vast, liquid billows.

In such a place it is difficult to believe that the world is actually peopled. It seems as if it might be the dark of the day after Cain killed Abel, and as if all of humanity's remainder was huddled in affright away from the awful spaciousness of Creation.

The night Ralph Hagadorn started out for Echo Bay — bent on a pleasant duty — he laughed to himself, and said that he did not at all object to being the only man in the world, so long as the world remained as unspeakably beautiful as it was when he buckled on his skates and shot away into the solitude. He was bent on reaching his best friend in time to act as groomsman, and business had delayed him till time was at its briefest. So he journeyed by night and journeyed alone, and when the tang of the frost got at his blood, he felt as a spirited horse feels when it gets free of bit and bridle. The ice was as glass, his skates were keen, his frame fit, and his venture to his taste! So he laughed, and cut through the air as a sharp stone cleaves the water. He could hear the whistling of the air as he cleft it.

As he went on and on in the black stillness, he began to have fancies. He imagined himself enormously tall — a great Viking of the Northland, hastening over icy fiords to his love. And that reminded him that he had a love — though, indeed, that thought was always present with him as a background for other thoughts. To be sure, he had not told her that she was his love, for he had seen her only a few times, and the auspicious occasion had not yet presented itself. She lived at Echo Bay also, and was to be the maid of honor to his friend's bride — which was one more reason why he skated almost as swiftly as the wind, and why, now and then, he let out a shout of exultation.

The one cloud that crossed Hagadorn's sun of expectancy was the knowledge that Marie Beaujeu's father had money, and that Marie lived in a house with two stories to it, and wore otter skin about her throat and little satin-lined mink boots on her feet when she went sledding. Moreover, in the locket in which she treasured a bit of her dead mother's hair, there was a black pearl as big as a pea. These things made it difficult — perhaps impossible — for Ralph Hagadorn to say more than, "I love you." But that much he meant to say though he were scourged with chagrin for his temerity.

This determination grew upon him as he swept along the ice under the starlight. Venus made a glowing path toward the west and seemed eager to reassure him. He was sorry he could not skim down that avenue of light which flowed from the love-star, but he was forced to turn his back upon it and face the black northeast.

It came to him with a shock that he was not alone. His eyelashes were frosted and his eyeballs blurred with the cold, so at first he thought it might be an illusion. But when he had rubbed his eyes hard, he made sure that not very far in front of him was a long white skater in fluttering garments who sped over the ice as fast as ever werewolf went.

He called aloud, but there was no answer. He shaped his hands and trumpeted through them, but the silence was as before — it was complete. So then he gave chase, setting his teeth hard and putting a tension on his firm young muscles. But go however he would, the white skater went faster. After a time, as he glanced at the cold gleam of the north star, he perceived that he was being led from his direct path. For a moment he hesitated, wondering if he would not better keep to his road, but his weird companion seemed to draw him on irresistibly, and finding it sweet to follow, he followed.

Of course it came to him more than once in that strange pursuit, that the white skater was no earthly guide. Up in those latitudes men see curious things when the hoar frost is on the earth. Hagadorn's own father — to hark no further than that for an instance! — who lived up there with the Lake Superior Indians, and worked in the copper mines, had welcomed a woman at his hut one bitter night, who was gone by morning, leaving wolf tracks on the snow! Yes, it was so, and John Fontanelle, the half-breed, could tell you about it any day — if he were alive. (Alack, the snow where the wolf tracks were, is melted now!)

Well, Hagadorn followed the white skater all the night, and when the ice flushed pink at dawn, and arrows of lovely light shot up into the cold heavens, she was gone, and Hagadorn was at his destination. The sun climbed arrogantly up to his place above all other things, and as Hagadorn took off his skates and glanced carelessly lakeward, he beheld a great wind-rift in the ice, and the waves showing blue and hungry between white fields. Had he rushed along his intended path, watching the stars to guide him, his glance turned upward, all his body at magnificent momentum, he must certainly have gone into that cold grave.

How wonderful that it had been sweet to follow the white skater, and that he followed!

His heart beat hard as he hurried to his friend's house. But he encountered no wedding furore. His friend met him as men meet in houses of mourning.

"Is this your wedding face?" cried Hagadorn. "Why, man, starved as I am, I look more like a bridegroom than you!"

"There's no wedding to-day!"

"No wedding! Why, you're not — "

"Marie Beaujeu died last night — "

"Marie — "

"Died last night. She had been skating in the afternoon, and she came home chilled and wandering in her mind, as if the frost had got in it somehow. She grew worse and worse, and all the time she talked of you."

"Of me?"

"We wondered what it meant. No one knew you were lovers."

"I didn't know it myself; more's the pity. At least, I didn't know — "

"She said you were on the ice, and that you didn't know about the big breaking-up, and she cried to us that the wind was off shore and the rift widening. She cried over and over again that you could come in by the old French creek if you only knew — "

"I came in that way."

"But how did you come to do that? It's out of the path. We thought perhaps — "

But Hagadorn broke in with his story and told him all as it had come to pass.

That day they watched beside the maiden, who lay with tapers at her head and at her feet, and in the little church the bride who might have been at her wedding said prayers for her friend. They buried Marie Beaujeu in her bridesmaid white, and Hagadorn was before the altar with her, as he had intended from the first! Then at midnight the lovers who were to wed whispered their vows in the gloom of the cold church, and walked together through the snow to lay their bridal wreaths upon a grave.

Three nights later, Hagadorn skated back again to his home. They wanted him to go by sunlight, but he had his way, and went when Venus made her bright path on the ice.

The truth was, he had hoped for the companionship of the white skater. But he did not have it. His only companion was the wind. The only voice he heard was the baying of a wolf on the north shore. The world was as empty and as white as if God had just created it, and the sun had not yet colored nor man defiled it.

THEIR DEAR LITTLE GHOST

THE first time one looked at Elsbeth, one was not prepossessed. She was thin and brown, her nose turned slightly upward, her toes went in just a perceptible degree, and her hair was perfectly straight. But when one looked longer, one perceived that she was a charming little creature. The straight hair was as fine as silk, and hung in funny little braids down her back; there was not a flaw in her soft brown skin, and her mouth was tender and shapely. But her particular charm lay in a look which she habitually had, of seeming to know curious things — such as it is not allotted to ordinary persons to know. One felt tempted to say to her:

"What are these beautiful things which you know, and of which others are ignorant? What is it you see with those wise and pellucid eyes? Why is it that everybody loves you?"

Elsbeth was my little godchild, and I knew her better than I knew any other child in the world. But still I could not truthfully say that I was familiar with her, for to me her spirit was like a fair and fragrant road in the midst of which I might walk in peace and joy, but where I was continually to discover something new. The last time I saw her quite well and strong was over in the woods where she had gone with her two little brothers and her nurse to pass the hottest weeks of summer. I followed her, foolish old creature that I was, just to be near her, for I needed to dwell where the sweet aroma of her life could reach me.

One morning when I came from my room, limping a little, because I am not so young as I used to be, and the lake wind works havoc with me, my little godchild came dancing to me singing:

"Come with me and I'll show you my places, my places, my places!"

Miriam, when she chanted by the Red Sea might have been more exultant, but she could not have been more bewitching. Of course I knew what "places" were, because I had once been a little girl myself, but unless you are acquainted with the real meaning of "places," it would be useless to try to explain. Either you know "places" or you do not — just as you understand the meaning of poetry or you do not. There are things in the world which cannot be taught.

Elsbeth's two tiny brothers were present, and I took one by each hand and followed her. No sooner had we got out of doors in the woods than a sort of mystery fell upon the world and upon us. We were cautioned to move silently, and we did so, avoiding the crunching of dry twigs.

"The fairies hate noise," whispered my little godchild, her eyes narrowing like a cat's.

"I must get my wand first thing I do," she said in an awed undertone. "It is useless to try to do anything without a wand."

The tiny boys were profoundly impressed, and, indeed, so was I. I felt that at last, I should, if I behaved properly, see the fairies, which had hitherto avoided my materialistic gaze. It was an enchanting moment, for there appeared, just then, to be nothing commonplace about life.

There was a swale near by, and into this the little girl plunged. I could see her red straw hat bobbing about among the tall rushes, and I wondered if there were snakes.

"Do you think there are snakes?" I asked one of the tiny boys.

"If there are," he said with conviction, "they won't dare hurt her."

He convinced me. I feared no more. Presently Elsbeth came out of the swale. In her hand was a brown "cattail," perfectly full and round. She carried it as queens carry their sceptres — the beautiful queens we dream of in our youth.

"Come," she commanded, and waved the sceptre in a fine manner. So we followed, each tiny boy gripping my hand tight. We were all three a trifle awed. Elsbeth led us into a dark underbrush. The branches, as they flew back in our faces, left them wet with dew. A wee path, made by the girl's dear feet, guided our footsteps. Perfumes of elderberry and wild cucumber scented the air. A bird, frightened from its nest, made frantic cries above our heads. The underbrush thickened. Presently the gloom of the hemlocks was over us, and in the midst of the shadowy green a tulip tree flaunted its leaves. Waves boomed and broke upon the shore below. There was a growing dampness as we went on, treading very lightly. A little green snake ran coquettishly from us. A fat and glossy squirrel chattered at us from a safe height, stroking his whiskers with a complaisant air.

At length we reached the "place." It was a circle of velvet grass, bright as the first blades of spring, delicate as fine sea-ferns. The sunlight, falling down the shaft between the hemlocks, flooded it with a softened light and made the forest round about look like deep purple velvet. My little godchild stood in the midst and raised her wand impressively.

"This is my place," she said, with a sort of wonderful gladness in her tone. "This is where I come to the fairy balls. Do you see them?"

"See what?" whispered one tiny boy.

"The fairies."

There was a silence. The older boy pulled at my skirt.

"Do YOU see them?" he asked, his voice trembling with expectancy.

"Indeed," I said, "I fear I am too old and wicked to see fairies, and yet — are their hats red?"

"They are," laughed my little girl. "Their hats are red, and as small — as small!" She held up the pearly nail of her wee finger to give us the correct idea.

"And their shoes are very pointed at the toes?"

"Oh, very pointed!"

"And their garments are green?"

"As green as grass."

"And they blow little horns?"

"The sweetest little horns!"

"I think I see them," I cried.

"We think we see them too," said the tiny boys, laughing in perfect glee.

"And you hear their horns, don't you?" my little godchild asked somewhat anxiously.

"Don't we hear their horns?" I asked the tiny boys.

"We think we hear their horns," they cried. "Don't you think we do?"

"It must be we do," I said. "Aren't we very, very happy?"

We all laughed softly. Then we kissed each other and Elsbeth led us out, her wand high in the air.

And so my feet found the lost path to Arcady.

The next day I was called to the Pacific coast, and duty kept me there till well into December. A few days before the date set for my return to my home, a letter came from Elsbeth's mother.

"Our little girl is gone into the Unknown," she wrote — "that Unknown in which she seemed to be forever trying to pry. We knew she was going, and we told her. She was quite brave, but she begged us to try some way to keep her till after Christmas. 'My presents are not finished yet,' she made moan. 'And I did so want to see what I was going to have. You can't have a very happy Christmas without me, I should think. Can you arrange to keep me somehow till after then?' We could not 'arrange' either with God in heaven or science upon earth, and she is gone."

She was only my little godchild, and I am an old maid, with no business fretting over children, but it seemed as if the medium of light and beauty had been taken from me. Through this crystal soul I had perceived whatever was loveliest. However, what was, was! I returned to my home and took up a course of Egyptian history, and determined to concern myself with nothing this side the Ptolemies.

Her mother has told me how, on Christmas eve, as usual, she and Elsbeth's father filled the stockings of the little ones, and hung them, where they had always hung, by the fireplace. They had little heart for the task, but they had been prodigal that year in their expenditures, and had heaped upon the two tiny boys all the treasures they thought would appeal to them. They asked themselves how they could have been so insane previously as to exercise economy at Christmas time, and what they meant by not getting Elsbeth the autoharp she had asked for the year before.

"And now — " began her father, thinking of harps. But he could not complete this sentence, of course, and the two went on passionately and almost angrily with their task. There were two stockings and two piles of toys. Two stockings only, and only two piles of toys! Two is very little!

They went away and left the darkened room,

and after a time they slept — after a long time. Perhaps that was about the time the tiny boys awoke, and, putting on their little dressing gowns and bed slippers, made a dash for the room where the Christmas things were always placed. The older one carried a candle which gave out a feeble light. The other followed behind through the silent house. They were very impatient and eager, but when they reached the door of the sitting-room they stopped, for they saw that another child was before them.

It was a delicate little creature, sitting in her white night gown, with two rumpled funny braids falling down her back, and she seemed to be weeping. As they watched, she arose, and putting out one slender finger as a child does when she counts, she made sure over and over again — three sad times — that there were only two stockings and two piles of toys! Only those and no more.

The little figure looked so familiar that the boys started toward it, but just then, putting up her arm and bowing her face in it, as Elsbeth had been used to do when she wept or was offended, the little thing glided away and went out. That's what the boys said. It went out as a candle goes out.

They ran and woke their parents with the tale, and all the house was searched in a wonderment, and disbelief, and hope, and tumult! But nothing was found. For nights they watched. But there was only the silent house. Only the empty rooms. They told the boys they must have been mistaken. But the boys shook their heads.

"We know our Elsbeth," said they. "It was our

Elsbeth, cryin' 'cause she hadn't no stockin' an' no toys, and we would have given her all ours, only she went out — jus' went out!"

Alack!

The next Christmas I helped with the little festival. It was none of my affair, but I asked to help, and they let me, and when we were all through there were three stockings and three piles of toys, and in the largest one was all the things that I could think of that my dear child would love. I locked the boys' chamber that night, and I slept on the divan in the parlor off the sitting-room. I slept but little, and the night was very still — so windless and white and still that I think I must have heard the slightest noise. Yet I heard none. Had I been in my grave I think my ears would not have remained more unsaluted.

Yet when daylight came and I went to unlock the boys' bedchamber door, I saw that the stocking and all the treasures which I had bought for my little godchild were gone. There was not a vestige of them remaining!

Of course we told the boys nothing. As for me, after dinner I went home and buried myself once more in my history, and so interested was I that midnight came without my knowing it. I should not have looked up at all, I suppose, to become aware of the time, had it not been for a faint, sweet sound as of a child striking a stringed instrument. It was so delicate and remote that I hardly heard it, but so joyous and tender that I could not but listen, and when I heard it a second time it seemed as if I caught the echo of a child's laugh. At first I was puzzled.

Then I remembered the little autoharp I had placed among the other things in that pile of vanished toys. I said aloud:

"Farewell, dear little ghost. Go rest. Rest in joy, dear little ghost. Farewell, farewell."

That was years ago, but there has been silence since. Elsbeth was always an obedient little thing.

A SPECTRAL COLLIE

WILLIAM PERCY CECIL happened to be a younger son, so he left home — which was England — and went to Kansas to ranch it. Thousands of younger sons do the same, only their destination is not invariably Kansas.

An agent at Wichita picked out Cecil's farm for him and sent the deeds over to England before Cecil left. He said there was a house on the place. So Cecil's mother fitted him out for America just as she had fitted out another superfluous boy for Africa, and parted from him with an heroic front and big agonies of mother-ache which she kept to herself.

The boy bore up the way a man of his blood ought, but when he went out to the kennel to see Nita, his collie, he went to pieces somehow, and rolled on the grass with her in his arms and wept like a booby. But the remarkable part of it was that Nita wept too, big, hot dog tears which her master wiped away. When he went off she howled like a hungry baby, and had to be switched before she would give any one a night's sleep.

When Cecil got over on his Kansas place he fitted up the shack as cosily as he could, and learned how to fry bacon and make soda biscuits. Incidentally, he did farming, and sunk a heap of money, finding out how not to do things. Meantime, the Americans laughed at him, and were inclined to turn the cold shoulder, and his compatriots, of whom there were a number in the county, did not prove to his liking. They consoled themselves for their exiled state in fashions not in keeping with Cecil's traditions. His homesickness went deeper than theirs, perhaps, and American whiskey could not make up for the loss of his English home, nor flirtations with the gay American village girls quite compensate him for the loss of his English mother. So he kept to himself and had nostalgia as some men have consumption.

At length the loneliness got so bad that he had to see some living thing from home, or make a flunk of it and go back like a cry baby. He had a stiff pride still, though he sobbed himself to sleep more than one night, as many a pioneer has done before him. So he wrote home for Nita, the collie, and got word that she would be sent. Arrangements were made for her care all along the line, and she was properly boxed and shipped.

As the time drew near for her arrival, Cecil could hardly eat. He was too excited to apply himself to anything. The day of her expected arrival he actually got up at five o'clock to clean the house and make it look as fine as possible for her inspection. Then he hitched up and drove fifteen miles to get her. The train pulled out just before he reached the station, so Nita in her box was waiting for him on the platform. He could see her in a queer way, as one sees the purple centre of a revolving circle of light; for, to tell the truth, with the long ride in the morning sun, and the beating of his heart, Cecil was only about half-conscious of anything. He wanted to yell, but he didn't. He kept himself in hand and lifted up the sliding side of the box and called to Nita, and she came out.

But it wasn't the man who fainted, though he might have done so, being crazy homesick as he was, and half-fed and overworked while he was yet soft from an easy life. No, it was the dog! She looked at her master's face, gave one cry of inexpressible joy, and fell over in a real feminine sort of a faint, and had to be brought to like any other lady, with camphor and water and a few drops of spirit down her throat. Then Cecil got up on the wagon seat, and she sat beside him with her head on his arm, and they rode home in absolute silence, each feeling too much for speech. After they reached home, however, Cecil showed her all over the place, and she barked out her ideas in glad sociability.

After that Cecil and Nita were inseparable. She walked beside him all day when he was out with the cultivator, or when he was mowing or reaping. She ate beside him at table and slept across his feet at night. Evenings when he looked over the Graphic from home, or read the books his mother sent him, that he might keep in touch with the world, Nita was beside him, patient, but jealous. Then, when he threw his book or paper down and took her on his knee and looked into her pretty eyes, or frolicked with her, she fairly laughed with delight.

In short, she was faithful with that faith of which only a dog is capable — that unquestioning faith to which even the most loving women never quite attain.

However, Fate was annoyed at this perfect friendship. It didn't give her enough to do, and Fate is a restless thing with a horrible appetite for variety.

So poor Nita died one day mysteriously, and gave her last look to Cecil as a matter of course; and he held her paws till the last moment, as a stanch friend should, and laid her away decently in a pine box in the cornfield, where he could be shielded from public view if he chose to go there now and then and sit beside her grave.

He went to bed very lonely, indeed, the first night. The shack seemed to him to be removed endless miles from the other habitations of men. He seemed cut off from the world, and ached to hear the cheerful little barks which Nita had been in the habit of giving him by way of good night. Her amiable eye with its friendly light was missing, the gay wag of her tail was gone; all her ridiculous ways, at which he was never tired of laughing, were things of the past.

He lay down, busy with these thoughts, yet so habituated to Nita's presence, that when her weight rested upon his feet, as usual, he felt no surprise. But after a moment it came to him that as she was dead the weight he felt upon his feet could not be hers. And yet, there it was, warm and comfortable, cuddling down in the familiar way. He actually sat up and put his hand down to the foot of the bed to discover what was there. But there was nothing there, save the weight. And that stayed with him that night and many nights after.

It happened that Cecil was a fool, as men will be when they are young, and he worked too hard, and didn't take proper care of himself; and so it came about that he fell sick with a low fever. He struggled around for a few days, trying to work it off, but one morning he awoke only to the consciousness of absurd dreams. He seemed to be on the sea, sailing for home, and the boat was tossing and pitching in a weary circle, and could make no headway. His heart was burning with impatience, but the boat went round and round in that endless circle till he shrieked out with agony.

The next neighbors were the Taylors, who lived two miles and a half away. They were awakened that morning by the howling of a dog before their door. It was a hideous sound and would give them no peace. So Charlie Taylor got up and opened the door, discovering there an excited little collie.

"Why, Tom," he called, "I thought Cecil's collie was dead!"

"She is," called back Tom.

"No, she ain't neither, for here she is, shakin' like an aspin, and a beggin' me to go with her. Come out, Tom, and see."

It was Nita, no denying, and the men, perplexed, followed her to Cecil's shack, where they found him babbling.

But that was the last of her. Cecil said he never felt her on his feet again. She had performed her final service for him, he said. The neighbors tried to laugh at the story at first, but they knew the Taylors wouldn't take the trouble to lie, and as for Cecil, no one would have ventured to chaff him.

THE HOUSE THAT WAS NOT

BART FLEMING took his bride out to his ranch on the plains when she was but seventeen years old, and the two set up housekeeping in three hundred and twenty acres of corn and rye. Off toward the west there was an unbroken sea of tossing corn at that time of the year when the bride came out, and as her sewing window was on the side of the house which faced the sunset, she passed a good part of each day looking into that great rustling mass, breathing in its succulent odors and listening to its sibilant melody. It was her picture gallery, her opera, her spectacle, and, being sensible, — or perhaps, being merely happy, — she made the most of it.

When harvesting time came and the corn was cut, she had much entertainment in discovering what lay beyond. The town was east, and it chanced that she had never ridden west. So, when the rolling hills of this newly beholden land lifted themselves for her contemplation, and the harvest sun, all in an angry and sanguinary glow sank in the veiled horizon, and at noon a scarf of golden vapor wavered up and down along the earth line, it was as if a new world had been made for her. Sometimes, at the coming of a storm, a whip-lash of purple cloud, full of electric agility, snapped along the western horizon.

"Oh, you'll see a lot of queer things on these here plains," her husband said when she spoke to him of these phenomena. "I guess what you see is the wind."

"The wind!" cried Flora. "You can't see the wind, Bart."

"Now look here, Flora," returned Bart, with benevolent emphasis, "you're a smart one, but you don't know all I know about this here country. I've lived here three mortal years, waitin' for you to git up out of your mother's arms and come out to keep me company, and I know what there is to know. Some things out here is queer — so queer folks wouldn't believe 'em unless they saw. An' some's so pig-headed they don't believe their own eyes. As for th' wind, if you lay down flat and squint toward th' west, you can see it blowin' along near th' ground, like a big ribbon; an' sometimes it's th' color of air, an' sometimes it's silver an' gold, an' sometimes, when a storm is comin', it's purple."

"If you got so tired looking at the wind, why didn't you marry some other girl, Bart, instead of waiting for me?"

Flora was more interested in the first part of Bart's speech than in the last.

"Oh, come on!" protested Bart, and he picked her up in his arms and jumped her toward the ceiling of the low shack as if she were a little girl — but then, to be sure, she wasn't much more.

Of all the things Flora saw when the corn was cut down, nothing interested her so much as a low cottage, something like her own, which lay away in the distance. She could not guess how far it might be, because distances are deceiving out there, where the altitude is high and the air is as clear as one of those mystic balls of glass in which the sallow mystics of India see the moving shadows of the future.

She had not known there were neighbors so near, and she wondered for several days about them before she ventured to say anything to Bart on the subject. Indeed, for some reason which she did not attempt to explain to herself, she felt shy about broaching the matter. Perhaps Bart did not want her to know the people. The thought came to her, as naughty thoughts will come, even to the best of persons, that some handsome young men might be "baching" it out there by themselves, and Bart didn't wish her to make their acquaintance. Bart had flattered her so much that she had actually begun to think herself beautiful, though as a matter of fact she was only a nice little girl with a lot of reddish-brown hair, and a bright pair of reddish-brown eyes in a white face.

"Bart," she ventured one evening, as the sun, at its fiercest, rushed toward the great black hollow of the west, "who lives over there in that shack?"

She turned away from the window where she had been looking at the incarnadined disk, and she thought she saw Bart turn pale. But then, her eyes were so blurred with the glory she had been gazing at, that she might easily have been mistaken.

"I say, Bart, why don't you speak? If there's any one around to associate with, I should think you'd let me have the benefit of their company. It isn't as funny as you think, staying here alone days and days."

"You ain't gettin' homesick, be you, sweet-heart?" cried Bart, putting his arms around her. "You ain't gettin' tired of my society, be yeh?"

It took some time to answer this question in a satisfactory manner, but at length Flora was able to return to her original topic.

"But the shack, Bart! Who lives there, anyway?"

"I'm not acquainted with 'em," said Bart, sharply. "Ain't them biscuits done, Flora?"

Then, of course, she grew obstinate.

"Those biscuits will never be done, Bart, till I know about that house, and why you never spoke of it, and why nobody ever comes down the road from there. Some one lives there I know, for in the mornings and at night I see the smoke coming out of the chimney."

"Do you now?" cried Bart, opening his eyes and looking at her with unfeigned interest. "Well, do you know, sometimes I've fancied I seen that too?"

"Well, why not," cried Flora, in half anger. "Why shouldn't you?"

"See here, Flora, take them biscuits out an' listen to me. There ain't no house there. Hello! I didn't know you'd go for to drop the biscuits. Wait, I'll help you pick 'em up. By cracky, they're hot, ain't they? What you puttin' a towel over 'em for? Well, you set down here on my knee, so. Now you look over at that there house. You see it, don't yeh? Well, it ain't there! No! I saw it the first week I was out here. I was jus' half dyin', thinkin' of you an' wonderin' why you didn't write. That was the time you was mad at me. So I rode over there one day — lookin' up company, so t' speak — and there wa'n't no house there. I spent all one Sunday lookin' for it. Then I spoke to Jim Geary about it. He laughed an' got a little white about th' gills, an' he said he guessed I'd have to look a good while before I found it. He said that there shack was an ole joke."

"Why — what — "

"Well, this here is th' story he tol' me. He said a man an' his wife come out here t' live an' put up that there little place. An' she was young, you know, an' kind o' skeery, and she got lonesome. It worked on her an' worked on her, an' one day she up an' killed the baby an' her husband an' herself. Th' folks found 'em and buried 'em right there on their own ground. Well, about two weeks after that, th' house was burned down. Don't know how. Tramps, maybe. Anyhow, it burned. At least, I guess it burned!"

"You guess it burned!"

"Well, it ain't there, you know."

"But if it burned the ashes are there."

"All right, girlie, they're there then. Now let's have tea."

This they proceeded to do, and were happy and cheerful all evening, but that didn't keep Flora from rising at the first flush of dawn and stealing out of the house. She looked away over west as she went to the barn and there, dark and firm against the horizon, stood the little house against the pellucid sky of morning. She got on Ginger's back — Ginger being her own yellow broncho — and set off at a hard pace for the house. It didn't appear to come any nearer, but the objects which had seemed to be beside it came closer into view, and Flora pressed on, with her mind steeled for anything. But as she approached the poplar windbreak which stood to the north of the house, the little shack waned like a shadow before her. It faded and dimmed before her eyes.

She slapped Ginger's flanks and kept him going, and she at last got him up to the spot. But there was nothing there. The bunch grass grew tall and rank and in the midst of it lay a baby's shoe. Flora thought of picking it up, but something cold in her veins withheld her. Then she grew angry, and set Ginger's head toward the place and tried to drive him over it. But the yellow broncho gave one snort of fear, gathered himself in a bunch, and then, all tense, leaping muscles, made for home as only a broncho can.

STORY OF AN OBSTINATE CORPSE

VIRGIL HOYT is a photographer's assistant up at St. Paul, and enjoys his work without being consumed by it. He has been in search of the picturesque all over the West and hundreds of miles to the north, in Canada, and can speak three or four Indian dialects and put a canoe through the rapids. That is to say, he is a man of adventure, and no dreamer. He can fight well and shoot better, and swim so as to put up a winning race with the Indian boys, and he can sit in the saddle all day and not worry about it to-morrow.

Wherever he goes, he carries a camera.

"The world," Hoyt is in the habit of saying to those who sit with him when he smokes his pipe, "was created in six days to be photographed. Man — and particularly woman — was made for the same purpose. Clouds are not made to give moisture nor trees to cast shade. They have been created in order to give the camera obscura something to do."

In short, Virgil Hoyt's view of the world is whimsical, and he likes to be bothered neither with the disagreeable nor the mysterious. That is the reason he loathes and detests going to a house of mourning to photograph a corpse. The bad taste of it offends him, but above all, he doesn't like the necessity of shouldering, even for a few moments, a part of the burden of sorrow which belongs to some one else. He dislikes sorrow, and would willingly canoe five hundred miles up the cold Canadian rivers to get rid of it. Nevertheless, as assistant photographer, it is often his duty to do this very kind of thing.

Not long ago he was sent for by a rich Jewish family to photograph the remains of the mother, who had just died. He was put out, but he was only an assistant, and he went. He was taken to the front parlor, where the dead woman lay in her coffin. It was evident to him that there was some excitement in the household, and that a discussion was going on. But Hoyt said to himself that it didn't concern him, and he therefore paid no attention to it.

The daughter wanted the coffin turned on end in order that the corpse might face the camera properly, but Hoyt said he could overcome the recumbent attitude and make it appear that the face was taken in the position it would naturally hold in life, and so they went out and left him alone with the dead.

The face of the deceased was a strong and positive one, such as may often be seen among Jewish matrons. Hoyt regarded it with some admiration, thinking to himself that she was a woman who had known what she wanted, and who, once having made up her mind, would prove immovable. Such a character appealed to Hoyt. He reflected that he might have married if only he could have found a woman with strength of character sufficient to disagree with him. There was a strand of hair out of place on the dead woman's brow, and he gently pushed it back. A bud lifted its head too high from among the roses on her breast and spoiled the contour of the chin, so he broke it off. He remembered these things later with keen distinctness, and that his hand touched her chill face two or three times in the making of his arrangements.

Then he took the impression, and left the house.

He was busy at the time with some railroad work, and several days passed before he found opportunity to develop the plates. He took them from the bath in which they had lain with a number of others, and went energetically to work upon them, whistling some very saucy songs he had learned of the guide in the Red River country, and trying to forget that the face which was presently to appear was that of a dead woman. He had used three plates as a precaution against accident, and they came up well. But as they developed, he became aware of the existence of something in the photograph which had not been apparent to his eye in the subject. He was irritated, and without attempting to face the mystery, he made a few prints and laid them aside, ardently hoping that by some chance they would never be called for.

However, as luck would have it, — and Hoyt's luck never had been good, — his employer asked one day what had become of those photographs. Hoyt tried to evade making an answer, but the effort was futile, and he had to get out the finished prints and exhibit them. The older man sat staring at them a long time.

"Hoyt," he said, "you're a young man, and very likely you have never seen anything like this before. But I have. Not exactly the same thing, perhaps, but similar phenomena have come my way a number of times since I went in the business, and I want to tell you there are things in heaven and earth not dreamt of — "

"Oh, I know all that tommy-rot," cried Hoyt, angrily, "but when anything happens I want to know the reason why and how it is done."

"All right," answered his employer, "then you might explain why and how the sun rises."

But he humored the young man sufficiently to examine with him the baths in which the plates were submerged, and the plates themselves. All was as it should be; but the mystery was there, and could not be done away with.

Hoyt hoped against hope that the friends of the dead woman would somehow forget about the photographs; but the idea was unreasonable, and one day, as a matter of course, the daughter appeared and asked to see the pictures of her mother.

"Well, to tell the truth," stammered Hoyt, "they didn't come out quite — quite as well as we could wish."

"But let me see them," persisted the lady. "I'd like to look at them anyhow."

"Well, now," said Hoyt, trying to be soothing, as he believed it was always best to be with women, — to tell the truth he was an ignoramus where women were concerned, — "I think it would be better if you didn't look at them. There are reasons why — " he ambled on like this, stupid man that he was, till the lady naturally insisted upon seeing the pictures without a moment's delay.

So poor Hoyt brought them out and placed them in her hand, and then ran for the water pitcher, and had to be at the bother of bathing her forehead to keep her from fainting.

For what the lady saw was this: Over face and flowers and the head of the coffin fell a thick veil, the edges of which touched the floor in some places. It covered the features so well that not a hint of them was visible.

"There was nothing over mother's face!" cried the lady at length.

"Not a thing," acquiesced Hoyt. "I know, because I had occasion to touch her face just before I took the picture. I put some of her hair back from her brow."

"What does it mean, then?" asked the lady.

"You know better than I. There is no explanation in science. Perhaps there is some in — in psychology."

"Well," said the young woman, stammering a little and coloring, "mother was a good woman, but she always wanted her own way, and she always had it, too."

"Yes."

"And she never would have her picture taken. She didn't admire her own appearance. She said no one should ever see a picture of her."

"So?" said Hoyt, meditatively. "Well, she's kept her word, hasn't she?"

The two stood looking at the photographs for a time. Then Hoyt pointed to the open blaze in the grate.

"Throw them in," he commanded. "Don't let your father see them — don't keep them yourself. They wouldn't be agreeable things to keep."

"That's true enough," admitted the lady. And she threw them in the fire. Then Virgil Hoyt brought out the plates and broke them before her eyes.

And that was the end of it — except that Hoyt sometimes tells the story to those who sit beside him when his pipe is lighted.

A CHILD OF THE RAIN

IT was the night that Mona Meeks, the dress-maker, told him she didn't love him. He couldn't believe it at first, because he had so long been accustomed to the idea that she did, and no matter how rough the weather or how irascible the passengers, he felt a song in his heart as he punched transfers, and rang his bell punch, and signalled the driver when to let people off and on.

Now, suddenly, with no reason except a woman's, she had changed her mind. He dropped in to see her at five o'clock, just before time for the night shift, and to give her two red apples he had been saving for her. She looked at the apples as if they were invisible and she could not see them, and standing in her disorderly little dressmaking parlor, with its cuttings and scraps and litter of fabrics, she said:

"It is no use, John. I shall have to work here like this all my life — work here alone. For I don't love you, John. No, I don't. I thought I did, but it is a mistake."

"You mean it?" asked John, bringing up the words in a great gasp.

"Yes," she said, white and trembling and putting out her hands as if to beg for his mercy. And then — big, lumbering fool — he turned around and strode down the stairs and stood at the corner in the beating rain waiting for his car. It came along at length, spluttering on the wet rails and spitting out blue fire, and he took his shift after a gruff "Good night" to Johnson, the man he relieved.

He was glad the rain was bitter cold and drove in his face fiercely. He rejoiced at the cruelty of the wind, and when it hustled pedestrians before it, lashing them, twisting their clothes, and threatening their equilibrium, he felt amused. He was pleased at the chill in his bones and at the hunger that tortured him. At least, at first he thought it was hunger till he remembered that he had just eaten. The hours passed confusedly. He had no consciousness of time. But it must have been late, — near midnight, — judging by the fact that there were few persons visible anywhere in the black storm, when he noticed a little figure sitting at the far end of the car. He had not seen the child when she got on, but all was so curious and wild to him that evening — he himself seemed to himself the most curious and the wildest of all things — that it was not surprising that he should not have observed the little creature.

She was wrapped in a coat so much too large that it had become frayed at the bottom from dragging on the pavement. Her hair hung in unkempt stringiness about her bent shoulders, and her feet were covered with old arctics, many sizes too big, from which the soles hung loose.

Beside the little figure was a chest of dark wood, with curiously wrought hasps. From this depended a stout strap by which it could be carried over the shoulders. John Billings stared in, fascinated by the poor little thing with its head sadly drooping upon its breast, its thin blue hands relaxed upon its lap, and its whole attitude so suggestive of hunger, loneliness, and fatigue, that he made up his mind he would collect no fare from it.

"It will need its nickel for breakfast," he said to himself. "The company can stand this for once. Or, come to think of it, I might celebrate my hard luck. Here's to the brotherhood of failures!" And he took a nickel from one pocket of his great-coat and dropped it in another, ringing his bell punch to record the transfer.

The car plunged along in the darkness, and the rain beat more viciously than ever in his face. The night was full of the rushing sound of the storm. Owing to some change of temperature the glass of the car became obscured so that the young conductor could no longer see the little figure distinctly, and he grew anxious about the child.

"I wonder if it's all right," he said to himself. "I never saw living creature sit so still."

He opened the car door, intending to speak with the child, but just then something went wrong with the lights. There was a blue and green flickering, then darkness, a sudden halting of the car, and a great sweep of wind and rain in at the door. When, after a moment, light and motion reasserted themselves, and Billings had got the door together, he turned to look at the little passenger. But the car was empty.

It was a fact. There was no child there — not even moisture on the seat where she had been sitting.

"Bill," said he, going to the front door and addressing the driver, "what became of that little kid in the old cloak?"

"I didn't see no kid," said Bill, crossly. "For Gawd's sake, close the door, John, and git that draught off my back."

"Draught!" said John, indignantly, "where's the draught?"

"You've left the hind door open," growled Bill, and John saw him shivering as a blast struck him and ruffled the fur on his bear-skin coat. But the door was not open, and yet John had to admit to himself that the car seemed filled with wind and a strange coldness.

However, it didn't matter. Nothing mattered! Still, it was as well no doubt to look under the seats just to make sure no little crouching figure was there, and so he did. But there was nothing. In fact, John said to himself, he seemed to be getting expert in finding nothing where there ought to be something.

He might have stayed in the car, for there was no likelihood of more passengers that evening, but somehow he preferred going out where the rain could drench him and the wind pommel him. How horribly tired he was! If there were only some still place away from the blare of the city where a man could lie down and listen to the sound of the sea or the storm — or if one could grow suddenly old and get through with the bother of living — or if —

The car gave a sudden lurch as it rounded a curve, and for a moment it seemed to be a mere chance whether Conductor Billings would stay on his platform or go off under those fire-spitting wheels. He caught instinctively at his brake, saved himself, and stood still for a moment, panting.

"I must have dozed," he said to himself.

Just then, dimly, through the blurred window, he saw again the little figure of the child, its head on its breast as before, its blue hands lying in its lap and the curious box beside it. John Billings felt a coldness beyond the coldness of the night run through his blood. Then, with a half-stifled cry, he threw back the door, and made a desperate spring at the corner where the eerie thing sat.

And he touched the green carpeting on the seat, which was quite dry and warm, as if no dripping, miserable little wretch had ever crouched there.

He rushed to the front door.

"Bill," he roared, "I want to know about that kid."

"What kid?"

"The same kid! The wet one with the old coat and the box with iron hasps! The one that's been sitting here in the car!"

Bill turned his surly face to confront the young conductor.

"You've been drinking, you fool," said he. "Fust thing you know you'll be reported."

The conductor said not a word. He went slowly and weakly back to his post and stood there the rest of the way leaning against the end of the car for support. Once or twice he muttered:

"The poor little brat!" And again he said, "So you didn't love me after all!"

He never knew how he reached home, but he sank to sleep as dying men sink to death. All the same, being a hearty young man, he was on duty again next day but one, and again the night was rainy and cold.

It was the last run, and the car was spinning along at its limit, when there came a sudden soft shock. John Billings knew what that meant. He had felt something of the kind once before. He turned sick for a moment, and held on to the brake. Then he summoned his courage and went around to the side of the car, which had stopped. Bill, the driver, was before him, and had a limp little figure in his arms, and was carrying it to the gaslight. John gave one look and cried:

"It's the same kid, Bill! The one I told you of!"

True as truth were the ragged coat dangling from the pitiful body, the little blue hands, the thin shoulders, the stringy hair, the big arctics on the feet. And in the road not far off was the curious chest of dark wood with iron hasps.

"She ran under the car deliberate!" cried Bill. "I yelled to her, but she looked at me and ran straight on!"

He was white in spite of his weather-beaten skin.

"I guess you wasn't drunk last night after all,

John," said he.

"You — you are sure the kid is — is there?" gasped John.

"Not so damned sure!" said Bill.

But a few minutes later it was taken away in a patrol wagon, and with it the little box with iron hasps.

THE ROOM OF THE EVIL THOUGHT

THEY called it the room of the Evil Thought. It was really the pleasantest room in the house, and when the place had been used as the rectory, was the minister's study. It looked out on a mournful clump of larches, such as may often be seen in the old-fashioned yards in Michigan, and these threw a tender gloom over the apartment.

There was a wide fireplace in the room, and it had been the young minister's habit to sit there hours and hours, staring ahead of him at the fire, and smoking moodily. The replenishing of the fire and of his pipe, it was said, would afford him occupation all the day long, and that was how it came about that his parochial duties were neglected so that, little by little, the people became dissatisfied with him, though he was an eloquent young man, who could send his congregation away drunk on his influence. However, the calmer pulsed among his parish began to whisper that it was indeed the influence of the young minister and not that of the Holy Ghost which they felt, and it was finally decided that neither animal magnetism nor hypnotism were good substitutes for religion. And so they let him go.

The new rector moved into a smart brick house on the other side of the church, and gave receptions and dinner parties, and was punctilious about making his calls. The people therefore liked him very much — so much that they raised the debt on the church and bought a chime of bells, in their enthusiasm. Every one was lighter of heart than under the ministration of the previous rector. A burden appeared to be lifted from the community. True, there were a few who confessed the new man did not give them the food for thought which the old one had done, but, then, the former rector had made them uncomfortable! He had not only made them conscious of the sins of which they were already guilty, but also of those for which they had the latent capacity. A strange and fatal man, whom women loved to their sorrow, and whom simple men could not understand! It was generally agreed that the parish was well rid of him.

"He was a genius," said the people in commiseration. The word was an uncomplimentary epithet with them.

When the Hanscoms moved in the house which had been the old rectory, they gave Grandma Hanscom the room with the fireplace. Grandma was well pleased. The roaring fire warmed her heart as well as her chill old body, and she wept with weak joy when she looked at the larches, because they reminded her of the house she had lived in when she was first married. All the forenoon of the first day she was busy putting things away in bureau drawers and closets, but by afternoon she was ready to sit down in her high-backed rocker and enjoy the comforts of her room.

She nodded a bit before the fire, as she usually did after luncheon, and then she awoke with an awful start and sat staring before her with such a look in her gentle, filmy old eyes as had never been there before. She did not move, except to rock slightly, and the Thought grew and grew till her face was disguised as by some hideous mask of tragedy.

By and by the children came pounding at the door.

"Oh, grandma, let us in, please. We want to see your new room, and mamma gave us some ginger cookies on a plate, and we want to give some to you."

The door gave way under their assaults, and the three little ones stood peeping in, waiting for permission to enter. But it did not seem to be their grandma — their own dear grandma — who arose and tottered toward them in fierce haste, crying:

"Away, away! Out of my sight! Out of my sight before I do the thing I want to do! Such a terrible thing! Send some one to me quick, children, children! Send some one quick!"

They fled with feet shod with fear, and their mother came, and Grandma Hanscom sank down and clung about her skirts and sobbed:

"Tie me, Miranda. Make me fast to the bed or the wall. Get some one to watch me. For I want to do an awful thing!"

They put the trembling old creature in bed, and she raved there all the night long and cried out to be held, and to be kept from doing the fearful thing, whatever it was — for she never said what it was.

The next morning some one suggested taking her in the sitting-room where she would be with the family. So they laid her on the sofa, hemmed around with cushions, and before long she was her quiet self again, though exhausted, naturally, with the tumult of the previous night. Now and then, as the children played about her, a shadow crept over her face — a shadow as of cold remembrance — and then the perplexed tears followed.

When she seemed as well as ever they put her back in her room. But though the fire glowed and the lamp burned, as soon as ever she was alone they heard her shrill cries ringing to them that the Evil Thought had come again. So Hal, who was home from college, carried her up to his room, which she seemed to like very well. Then he went down to have a smoke before grandma's fire.

The next morning he was absent from breakfast. They thought he might have gone for an early walk, and waited for him a few minutes. Then his sister went to the room that looked upon the larches, and found him dressed and pacing the floor with a face set and stern. He had not been in bed at all, as she saw at once. His eyes were bloodshot, his face stricken as if with old age or sin or — but she could not make it out. When he saw her he sank in a chair and covered his face with his hands, and between the trembling fingers she could see drops of perspiration on his forehead.

"Hal!" she cried, "Hal, what is it?"

But for answer he threw his arms about the little table and clung to it, and looked at her with tortured eyes, in which she fancied she saw a gleam of hate. She ran, screaming, from the room, and her father came and went up to him and laid his hands on the boy's shoulders. And then a fearful thing happened.

All the family saw it. There could be no mistake. Hal's hands found their way with frantic eagerness toward his father's throat as if they would choke him, and the look in his eyes was so like a madman's that his father raised his fist and felled him as he used to fell men years before in the college fights, and then dragged him into the sitting-room and wept over him.

By evening, however, Hal was all right, and the family said it must have been a fever, — perhaps from overstudy, — at which Hal covertly smiled. But his father was still too anxious about him to let him out of his sight, so he put him on a cot in his room, and thus it chanced that the mother and Grace concluded to sleep together downstairs.

The two women made a sort of festival of it, and drank little cups of chocolate before the fire, and undid and brushed their brown braids, and smiled at each other, understandingly, with that sweet intuitive sympathy which women have, and Grace told her mother a number of things which she had been waiting for just such an auspicious occasion to confide.

But the larches were noisy and cried out with wild voices, and the flame of the fire grew blue and swirled about in the draught sinuously, so that a chill crept upon the two. Something cold appeared to envelop them — such a chill as pleasure voyagers feel when a berg steals beyond Newfoundland and glows blue and threatening upon their ocean path.

Then came something else which was not cold, but hot as the flames of hell — and they saw red, and stared at each other with maddened eyes, and then ran together from the room and clasped in close embrace safe beyond the fatal place, and thanked God they had not done the thing that they dared not speak of — the thing which suddenly came to them to do.

So they called it the room of the Evil Thought. They could not account for it. They avoided the thought of it, being healthy and happy folk. But none entered it more. The door was locked.

One day, Hal, reading the paper, came across a paragraph concerning the young minister who had once lived there, and who had thought and written there and so influenced the lives of those about him that they remembered him even while they disapproved.

"He cut a man's throat on board ship for Australia," said he, "and then he cut his own, without fatal effect — and jumped overboard, and so ended it. What a strange thing!"

Then they all looked at one another with subtle looks, and a shadow fell upon them and stayed the blood at their hearts.

The next week the room of the Evil Thought was pulled down to make way for a pansy bed, which is quite gay and innocent, and blooms all the better because the larches, with their eternal murmuring, have been laid low and carted away to the sawmill.

STORY OF THE VANISHING PATIENT

THERE had always been strange stories about the house, but it was a sensible, comfortable sort of a neighborhood, and people took pains to say to one another that there was nothing in these tales — of course not! Absolutely nothing! How could there be? It was a matter of common remark, however, that considering the amount of money the Nethertons had spent on the place, it was curious they lived there so little. They were nearly always away, — up North in the summer and down South in the winter, and over to Paris or London now and then, — and when they did come home it was only to entertain a number of guests from the city. The place was either plunged in gloom or gayety. The old gardener who kept house by himself in the cottage at the back of the yard had things much his own way by far the greater part of the time.

Dr. Block and his wife lived next door to the Nethertons, and he and his wife, who were so absurd as to be very happy in each other's company, had the benefit of the beautiful yard. They walked there mornings when the leaves were silvered with dew, and evenings they sat beside the lily pond and listened for the whip-poor-will. The doctor's wife moved her room over to that side of the house which commanded a view of the yard, and thus made the honeysuckles and laurel and clematis and all the masses of tossing greenery her own. Sitting there day after day with her sewing, she speculated about the mystery which hung impalpably yet undeniably over the house.

It happened one night when she and her husband had gone to their room, and were congratulating themselves on the fact that he had no very sick patients and was likely to enjoy a good night's rest, that a ring came at the door.

"If it's any one wanting you to leave home," warned his wife, "you must tell them you are all worn out. You've been disturbed every night this week, and it's too much!"

The young physician went downstairs. At the door stood a man whom he had never seen before.

"My wife is lying very ill next door," said the stranger, "so ill that I fear she will not live till morning. Will you please come to her at once?"

"Next door?" cried the physician. "I didn't know the Nethertons were home!"

"Please hasten," begged the man. "I must go back to her. Follow as quickly as you can."

The doctor went back upstairs to complete his toilet.

"How absurd," protested his wife when she heard the story. "There is no one at the Nethertons'. I sit where I can see the front door, and no one can enter without my knowing it, and I have been sewing by the window all day. If there were any one in the house, the gardener would have the porch lantern lighted. It is some plot. Some one has designs on you. You must not go."

But he went. As he left the room his wife placed a revolver in his pocket.

The great porch of the mansion was dark, but the physician made out that the door was open, and he entered. A feeble light came from the bronze lamp at the turn of the stairs, and by it he found his way, his feet sinking noiselessly in the rich carpets. At the head of the stairs the man met him. The doctor thought himself a tall man, but the stranger topped him by half a head. He motioned the physician to follow him, and the two went down the hall to the front room. The place was flushed with a rose-colored glow from several lamps. On a silken couch, in the midst of pillows, lay a woman dying with consumption. She was like a lily, white, shapely, graceful, with feeble yet charming movements. She looked at the doctor appealingly, then, seeing in his eyes the involuntary verdict that her hour was at hand, she turned toward her companion with a glance of anguish. Dr. Block asked a few questions. The man answered them, the woman remaining silent. The physician administered something stimulating, and then wrote a prescription which he placed on the mantel-shelf.

"The drug store is closed to-night," he said, "and I fear the druggist has gone home. You can have the prescription filled the first thing in the morning, and I will be over before breakfast."

After that, there was no reason why he should not have gone home. Yet, oddly enough, he preferred to stay. Nor was it professional anxiety that prompted this delay. He longed to watch those mysterious persons, who, almost oblivious of his presence, were speaking their mortal farewells in their glances, which were impassioned and of unutterable sadness.

He sat as if fascinated. He watched the glitter of rings on the woman's long, white hands, he noted the waving of light hair about her temples, he observed the details of her gown of soft white silk which fell about her in voluminous folds. Now and then the man gave her of the stimulant which the doctor had provided; sometimes he bathed her face with water. Once he paced the floor for a moment till a motion of her hand quieted him.

After a time, feeling that it would be more sensible and considerate of him to leave, the doctor made his way home. His wife was awake, impatient to hear of his experiences. She listened to his tale in silence, and when he had finished she turned her face to the wall and made no comment.

"You seem to be ill, my dear," he said. "You have a chill. You are shivering."

"I have no chill," she replied sharply. "But I — well, you may leave the light burning."

The next morning before breakfast the doctor crossed the dewy sward to the Netherton house. The front door was locked, and no one answered to his repeated ringings. The old gardener chanced to be cutting the grass near at hand, and he came running up.

"What you ringin' that door-bell for, doctor?" said he. "The folks ain't come home yet. There ain't nobody there."

"Yes, there is, Jim. I was called here last night. A

man came for me to attend his wife. They must both have fallen asleep that the bell is not answered. I wouldn't be surprised to find her dead, as a matter of fact. She was a desperately sick woman. Perhaps she is dead and something has happened to him. You have the key to the door, Jim. Let me in."

But the old man was shaking in every limb, and refused to do as he was bid.

"Don't you never go in there, doctor," whispered he, with chattering teeth. "Don't you go for to 'tend no one. You jus' come tell me when you sent for that way. No, I ain't goin' in, doctor, nohow. It ain't part of my duties to go in. That's been stipulated by Mr. Netherton. It's my business to look after the garden."

Argument was useless. Dr. Block took the bunch of keys from the old man's pocket and himself unlocked the front door and entered. He mounted the steps and made his way to the upper room. There was no evidence of occupancy. The place was silent, and, so far as living creature went, vacant. The dust lay over everything. It covered the delicate damask of the sofa where he had seen the dying woman. It rested on the pillows. The place smelled musty and evil, as if it had not been used for a long time. The lamps of the room held not a drop of oil.

But on the mantel-shelf was the prescription which the doctor had written the night before. He read it, folded it, and put it in his pocket.

As he locked the outside door the old gardener came running to him.

"Don't you never go up there again, will you?" he pleaded, "not unless you see all the Nethertons home and I come for you myself. You won't, doctor?"

"No," said the doctor.

When he told his wife she kissed him, and said:

"Next time when I tell you to stay at home, you must stay!"

THE PIANO NEXT DOOR

BABETTE had gone away for the summer; the furniture was in its summer linens; the curtains were down, and Babette's husband, John Boyce, was alone in the house. It was the first year of his marriage, and he missed Babette. But then, as he often said to himself, he ought never to have married her. He did it from pure selfishness, and because he was determined to possess the most illusive, tantalizing, elegant, and utterly unmoral little creature that the sun shone upon. He wanted her because she reminded him of birds, and flowers, and summer winds, and other exquisite things created for the delectation of mankind. He neither expected nor desired her to think. He had half-frightened her into marrying him, had taken her to a poor man's home, provided her with no society such as she had been accustomed to, and he had no reasonable cause of complaint when she answered the call of summer and flitted away, like a butterfly in the morning sunshine, to the place where the flowers grew.

He wrote to her every evening, sitting in the stifling, ugly house, and poured out his soul as if it were a libation to a goddess. She sometimes answered by telegraph, sometimes by a perfumed note. He schooled himself not to feel hurt. Why should Babette write? Does a goldfinch indict epistles; or a humming-bird study composition; or a glancing, red-scaled fish in summer shallows consider the meaning of words?

He knew at the beginning what Babette was — guessed her limitations — trembled when he buttoned her tiny glove — kissed her dainty slipper when he found it in the closet after she was gone — thrilled at the sound of her laugh, or the memory of it! That was all. A mere case of love. He was in bonds. Babette was not. Therefore he was in the city, working overhours to pay for Babette's pretty follies down at the seaside. It was quite right and proper. He was a grub in the furrow; she a lark in the blue. Those had always been and always must be their relative positions.

Having attained a mood of philosophic calm, in which he was prepared to spend his evenings alone — as became a grub — and to await with dignified patience the return of his wife, it was in the nature of an inconsistency that he should have walked the floor of the dull little drawing-room like a lion in cage. It did not seem in keeping with the position of superior serenity which he had assumed, that, reading Babette's notes, he should have raged with jealousy, or that, in the loneliness of his unkempt chamber, he should have stretched out arms of longing. Even if Babette had been present, she would only have smiled her gay little smile and coquetted with him. She could not understand. He had known, of course, from the first moment, that she could not understand! And so, why the ache, ache, ache of the heart! Or WAS it the heart, or the brain, or the soul?

Sometimes, when the evenings were so hot that he could not endure the close air of the house, he sat on the narrow, dusty front porch and looked about him at his neighbors. The street had once been smart and aspiring, but it had fallen into decay and dejection. Pale young men, with flurried-looking wives, seemed to Boyce to occupy most of the houses. Sometimes three or four couples would live in one house. Most of these appeared to be childless. The women made a pretence at fashionable dressing, and wore their hair elaborately in fashions which somehow suggested boarding-houses to Boyce, though he could not have told why. Every house in the block needed fresh paint. Lacking this renovation, the householders tried to make up for it by a display of lace curtains which, at every window, swayed in the smoke-weighted breeze. Strips of carpeting were laid down the front steps of the houses where the communities of young couples lived, and here, evenings, the inmates of the houses gathered, committing mild extravagances such as the treating of each other to ginger ale, or beer, or ice-cream.

Boyce watched these tawdry makeshifts at sociability with bitterness and loathing. He wondered how he could have been such a fool as to bring his exquisite Babette to this neighborhood. How could he expect that she would return to him? It was not reasonable. He ought to go down on his knees with gratitude that she even condescended to write him.

Sitting one night till late, — so late that the fashionable young wives with their husbands had retired from the strips of stair carpeting, — and raging at the loneliness which ate at his heart like a cancer, he heard, softly creeping through the windows of the house adjoining his own, the sound of comfortable melody.

It breathed upon his ear like a spirit of consolation, speaking of peace, of love which needs no reward save its own sweetness, of aspiration which looks forever beyond the thing of the hour to find attainment in that which is eternal. So insidiously did it whisper these things, so delicately did the simple and perfect melodies creep upon the spirit — that Boyce felt no resentment, but from the first listened as one who listens to learn, or as one who, fainting on the hot road, hears, far in the ferny deeps below, the gurgle of a spring.

Then came harmonies more intricate: fair fabrics of woven sound, in the midst of which gleamed golden threads of joy; a tapestry of sound, multi-tinted, gallant with story and achievement, and beautiful things. Boyce, sitting on his absurd piazza, with his knees jambed against the balustrade, and his chair back against the dun-colored wall of his house, seemed to be walking in the cathedral of the redwood forest, with blue above him, a vast hymn in his ears, pungent perfume in his nostrils, and mighty shafts of trees lifting themselves to heaven, proud and erect as pure men before their Judge. He stood on a mountain at sunrise, and saw the marvels of the amethystine clouds below his feet, heard an eternal and white silence, such as broods among the ever-lasting snows, and saw an eagle winging for the sun. He was in a city, and away from him, diverging like the spokes of a wheel, ran thronging streets, and to his sense came the beat, beat, beat of the city's heart. He saw the golden alchemy of a chosen race; saw greed transmitted to progress; saw that which had enslaved men, work at last to their liberation; heard the roar of mighty mills, and on the streets all the peoples of earth walking with common purpose, in fealty and understanding. And then, from the swelling of this concourse of great sounds, came a diminuendo, calm as philosophy, and from that, nothingness.

Boyce sat still for a long time, listening to the echoes which this music had awakened in his soul. He retired, at length, content, but determined that upon the morrow he would watch — the day being Sunday — for the musician who had so moved and taught him.

He arose early, therefore, and having prepared his own simple breakfast of fruit and coffee, took his station by the window to watch for the man. For he felt convinced that the exposition he had heard was that of a masculine mind. The long, hot hours of the morning went by, but the front door of the house next to his did not open.

"These artists sleep late," he complained. Still he watched. He was too much afraid of losing him to go out for dinner. By three in the afternoon he had grown impatient. He went to the house next door and rang the bell. There was no response. He thundered another appeal. An old woman with a cloth about her head answered the door. She was very deaf, and Boyce had difficulty in making himself understood.

"The family is in the country," was all she would say. "The family will not be home till September."

"But there is some one living here?" shouted Boyce.

"*I* live here," she said with dignity, putting back a wisp of dirty gray hair behind her ear. "It is my house. I sublet to the family."

"What family?"

But the old creature was not communicative.

"The family that lives here," she said.

"Then who plays the piano in this house?" roared Boyce. "Do you?"

He thought a shade of pallor showed itself on her ash-colored cheeks. Yet she smiled a little at the idea of her playing.

"There is no piano," she said, and she put an enigmatical emphasis to the words.

"Nonsense," cried Boyce, indignantly. "I heard a piano being played in this very house for hours last night!"

"You may enter," said the old woman, with an accent more vicious than hospitable.

Boyce almost burst into the drawing-room. It was a dusty and forbidding place, with ugly furniture and gaudy walls. No piano nor any other musical instrument stood in it. The intruder turned an angry and baffled face to the old woman, who was smiling with ill-concealed exultation.

"I shall see the other rooms," he announced. The old woman did not appear to be surprised at his impertinence.

"As you please," she said.

So, with the hobbling creature, with her bandaged head, for a guide, he explored every room of the house, which being identical with his own, he could do without fear of leaving any apartment unentered. But no piano did he find!

"Explain," roared Boyce at length, turning upon the leering old hag beside him. "Explain! For surely I heard music more beautiful than I can tell."

"I know nothing," she said. "But it is true I once had a lodger who rented the front room, and that he played upon the piano. I am poor at hearing, but he must have played well, for all the neighbors used to come in front of the house to listen, and sometimes they applauded him, and sometimes they were still. I could tell by watching their hands. Sometimes little children came and danced. Other times young men and women came and listened. But the young man died. The neighbors were angry. They came to look at him and said he had starved to death. It was no fault of mine. I sold his piano to pay his funeral expenses — and it took every cent to pay for them too, I'd have you know. But since then, sometimes — still, it must be nonsense, for I never heard it — folks say that he plays the piano in my room. It has kept me out of the letting of it more than once. But the family doesn't seem to mind — the family that lives here, you know. They will be back in September. Yes."

Boyce left her nodding her thanks at what he had placed in her hand, and went home to write it all to Babette — Babette who would laugh so merrily when she read it!

AN ASTRAL ONION

WHEN Tig Braddock came to Nora Finnegan he was red-headed and freckled, and, truth to tell, he remained with these features to the end of his life — a life prolonged by a lucky, if somewhat improbable, incident, as you shall hear.

Tig had shuffled off his parents as saurians, of some sorts, do their skins. During the temporary absence from home of his mother, who was at the bridewell, and the more extended vacation of his father, who, like Villon, loved the open road and the life of it, Tig, who was not a well-domesticated animal, wandered away. The humane society never heard of him, the neighbors did not miss him, and the law took no cognizance of this detached citizen — this lost pleiad. Tig would have sunk into that melancholy which is attendant upon hunger, — the only form of despair which babyhood knows, — if he had not wandered across the path of Nora Finnegan. Now Nora shone with steady brightness in her orbit, and no sooner had Tig entered her atmosphere, than he was warmed and comforted. Hunger could not live where Nora was. The basement room where she kept house was redolent with savory smells; and in the stove in her front room — which was also her bedroom — there was a bright fire glowing when fire was needed.

Nora went out washing for a living. But she was not a poor washerwoman. Not at all. She was a washerwoman triumphant. She had perfect health, an enormous frame, an abounding enthusiasm for life, and a rich abundance of professional pride. She believed herself to be the best washer of white clothes she had ever had the pleasure of knowing, and the value placed upon her services, and her long connection with certain families with large weekly washings, bore out this estimate of herself — an estimate which she never endeavored to conceal.

Nora had buried two husbands without being unduly depressed by the fact. The first husband had been a disappointment, and Nora winked at Providence when an accident in a tunnel carried him off — that is to say, carried the husband off. The second husband was not so much of a disappointment as a surprise. He developed ability of a literary order, and wrote songs which sold and made him a small fortune. Then he ran away with another woman. The woman spent his fortune, drove him to dissipation, and when he was dying he came back to Nora, who received him cordially, attended him to the end, and cheered his last hours by singing his own songs to him. Then she raised a headstone recounting his virtues, which were quite numerous, and refraining from any reference to those peculiarities which had caused him to be such a surprise.

Only one actual chagrin had ever nibbled at the sound heart of Nora Finnegan — a cruel chagrin, with long, white teeth, such as rodents have! She had never held a child to her breast, nor laughed in its eyes; never bathed the pink form of a little son or daughter; never felt a tugging of tiny hands at her voluminous calico skirts! Nora had burnt many candles before the statue of the blessed Virgin without remedying this deplorable condition. She had sent up unavailing prayers — she had, at times, wept hot tears of longing and loneliness. Sometimes in her sleep she dreamed that a wee form, warm and exquisitely soft, was pressed against her firm body, and that a hand with tiniest pink nails crept within her bosom. But as she reached out to snatch this delicious little creature closer, she woke to realize a barren woman's grief, and turned herself in anguish on her lonely pillow.

So when Tig came along, accompanied by two curs, who had faithfully followed him from his home, and when she learned the details of his story, she took him in, curs and all, and, having bathed the three of them, made them part and parcel of her home. This was after the demise of the second husband, and at a time when Nora felt that she had done all a woman could be expected to do for Hymen.

Tig was a preposterous baby. The curs were preposterous curs. Nora had always been afflicted with a surplus amount of laughter — laughter which had difficulty in attaching itself to anything, owing to the lack of the really comic in the surroundings of the poor. But with a red-headed and freckled baby boy and two trick dogs in the house, she found a good and sufficient excuse for her hilarity, and would have torn the cave where echo lies with her mirth, had that cave not been at such an immeasurable distance from the crowded neighborhood where she lived.

At the age of four Tig went to free kindergarten; at the age of six he was in school, and made three grades the first year and two the next. At fifteen he was graduated from the high school and went to work as errand boy in a newspaper office, with the fixed determination to make a journalist of himself.

Nora was a trifle worried about his morals when she discovered his intellect, but as time went on, and Tig showed no devotion for any woman save herself, and no consciousness that there were such things as bad boys or saloons in the world, she began to have confidence. All of his earnings were brought to her. Every holiday was spent with her. He told her his secrets and his aspirations. He admitted that he expected to become a great man, and, though he had not quite decided upon the nature of his career, — saving, of course, the makeshift of journalism, — it was not unlikely that he would elect to be a novelist like — well, probably like Thackeray.

Hope, always a charming creature, put on her most alluring smiles for Tig, and he made her his mistress, and feasted on the light of her eyes. Moreover, he was chaperoned, so to speak, by Nora Finnegan, who listened to every line Tig wrote, and made a mighty applause, and filled him up with good Irish stew, many colored as the coat of Joseph, and pungent with the inimitable perfume of "the rose of the cellar." Nora Finnegan understood the onion, and used it lovingly. She perceived the difference between the use and abuse of this pleasant and obvious friend of hungry man, and employed it with enthusiasm, but discretion. Thus it came about that whoever ate of her dinners, found the meals of other cooks strangely lacking in savor, and remembered with regret the soups and stews, the broiled steaks, and stuffed chickens of the woman who appreciated the onion.

When Nora Finnegan came home with a cold one day, she took it in such a jocular fashion that Tig felt not the least concern about her, and when, two days later, she died of pneumonia, he almost thought, at first, that it must be one of her jokes. She had departed with decision, such as had character-ized every act of her life, and had made as little trouble for others as possible. When she was dead the community had the opportunity of discovering the number of her friends. Miserable children with faces which revealed two generations of hunger, homeless boys with vicious countenances, miserable wrecks of humanity, women with bloated faces, came to weep over Nora's bier, and to lay a flower there, and to scuttle away, more abjectly lonely than even sin could make them. If the cats and the dogs, the sparrows and horses to which she had shown kindness, could also have attended her funeral, the procession would have been, from a point of num-bers, one of the most imposing the city had ever known. Tig used up all their savings to bury her, and the next week, by some peculiar fatality, he had a falling out with the night editor of his paper, and was discharged. This sank deep into his sensitive soul, and he swore he would be an underling no longer — which foolish resolution was directly traceable to his hair, the color of which, it will be recollected, was red.

Not being an underling, he was obliged to make himself into something else, and he recurred pas-sionately to his old idea of becoming a novelist. He settled down in Nora's basement rooms, went to work on a battered type-writer, did his own cooking, and occasionally pawned something to keep him in food. The environment was calculated to further impress him with the idea of his genius.

A certain magazine offered an alluring prize for a short story, and Tig wrote one, and rewrote it, making alterations, revisions, annotations, and inter-lineations which would have reflected credit upon Honoré; Balzac himself. Then he wrought all to-gether, with splendid brevity and dramatic force, — Tig's own words, — and mailed the same. He was convinced he would get the prize. He was just as much convinced of it as Nora Finnegan would have been if she had been with him.

So he went about doing more fiction, taking no especial care of himself, and wrapt in rosy dreams, which, not being warm enough for the weather, permitted him to come down with rheumatic fever.

He lay alone in his room and suffered such tor-ments as the condemned and rheumatic know, de-pending on one of Nora's former friends to come in twice a day and keep up the fire for him. This friend was aged ten, and looked like a sparrow who had been in a cyclone, but somewhere inside his bones was a wit which had spelled out devotion. He found fuel for the cracked stove, somehow or other. He brought it in a dirty sack which he carried on his back, and he kept warmth in Tig's miserable body. Moreover, he found food of a sort — cold, horrible bits often, and Tig wept when he saw them, remem-bering the meals Nora had served him.

Tig was getting better, though he was conscious

of a weak heart and a lamenting stomach, when, to his amazement, the Sparrow ceased to visit him. Not for a moment did Tig suspect desertion. He knew that only something in the nature of an act of Providence, as the insurance companies would designate it, could keep the little bundle of bones away from him. As the days went by, he became convinced of it, for no Sparrow came, and no coal lay upon the hearth. The basement window fortunately looked toward the south, and the pale April sunshine was beginning to make itself felt, so that the temperature of the room was not unbearable. But Tig languished; sank, sank, day by day, and was kept alive only by the conviction that the letter announcing the award of the thousand-dollar prize would presently come to him. One night he reached a place, where, for hunger and dejection, his mind wandered, and he seemed to be complaining all night to Nora of his woes. When the chill dawn came, with chittering of little birds on the dirty pavement, and an agitation of the scrawny willow "pussies," he was not able to lift his hand to his head. The window before his sight was but "a glimmering square." He said to himself that the end must be at hand. Yet it was cruel, cruel, with fame and fortune so near! If only he had some food, he might summon strength to rally — just for a little while! Impossible that he should die! And yet without food there was no choice.

Dreaming so of Nora's dinners, thinking how one spoonful of a stew such as she often compounded would now be his salvation, he became conscious of the presence of a strong perfume in the room. It was so familiar that it seemed like a subconsciousness, yet he found no name for this friendly odor for a bewildered minute or two. Little by little, however, it grew upon him, that it was the onion — that fragrant and kindly bulb which had attained its apotheosis in the cuisine of Nora Finnegan of sacred memory. He opened his languid eyes, to see if, mayhap, the plant had not attained some more palpable materialization.

Behold, it was so! Before him, in a brown earthen dish, — a most familiar dish, — was an onion, pearly white, in placid seas of gravy, smoking and delectable. With unexpected strength he raised himself, and reached for the dish, which floated before him in a halo made by its own steam. It moved toward him, offered a spoon to his hand, and as he ate he heard about the room the rustle of Nora Finnegan's starched skirts, and now and then a faint, faint echo of her old-time laugh — such an echo as one may find of the sea in the heart of a shell.

The noble bulb disappeared little by little before his voracity, and in contentment greater than virtue can give, he sank back upon his pillow and slept.

Two hours later the postman knocked at the door, and receiving no answer, forced his way in. Tig, half awake, saw him enter with no surprise. He felt no surprise when he put a letter in his hand bearing the name of the magazine to which he had sent his short story. He was not even surprised, when, tearing it open with suddenly alert hands, he found within the check for the first prize — the check he had expected.

All that day, as the April sunlight spread itself

upon his floor, he felt his strength grow. Late in the afternoon the Sparrow came back, paler, and more bony than ever, and sank, breathing hard, upon the floor, with his sack of coal.

"I've been sick," he said, trying to smile. "Terrible sick, but I come as soon as I could."

"Build up the fire," cried Tig, in a voice so strong it made the Sparrow start as if a stone had struck him. "Build up the fire, and forget you are sick. For, by the shade of Nora Finnegan, you shall be hungry no more!"

FROM THE LOOM OF THE DEAD

WHEN Urda Bjarnason tells a tale all the men stop their talking to listen, for they know her to be wise with the wisdom of the old people, and that she has more learning than can be got even from the great schools at Reykjavik. She is especially prized by them here in this new country where the Icelandmen are settled — this America, so new in letters, where the people speak foolishly and write unthinking books. So the men who know that it is given to the mothers of earth to be very wise, stop their six part singing, or their jangles about the free-thinkers, and give attentive ear when Urda Bjarnason lights her pipe and begins her tale.

She is very old. Her daughters and sons are all dead, but her granddaughter, who is most respectable, and the cousin of a physician, says that Urda is twenty-four and a hundred, and there are others who say that she is older still. She watches all that the Iceland people do in the new land; she knows about the building of the five villages on the North Dakota plain, and of the founding of the churches and the schools, and the tilling of the wheat farms. She notes with suspicion the actions of the women who bring home webs of cloth from the store, instead of spinning them as their mothers did before them; and she shakes her head at the wives who run to the village grocery store every fortnight, imitating the wasteful American women, who throw butter in the fire faster than it can be turned from the churn.

She watches yet other things. All winter long the white snows reach across the gently rolling plains as far as the eye can behold. In the morning she sees them tinted pink at the east; at noon she notes golden lights flashing across them; when the sky is gray — which is not often — she notes that they grow as ashen as a face with the death shadow on it. Sometimes they glitter with silver-like tips of ocean waves. But at these things she looks only casually. It is when the blue shadows dance on the snow that she leaves her corner behind the iron stove, and stands before the window, resting her two hands on the stout bar of her cane, and gazing out across the waste with eyes which age has restored after four decades of decrepitude.

The young Icelandmen say:

"Mother, it is the clouds hurrying across the sky that make the dance of the shadows."

"There are no clouds," she replies, and points to the jewel-like blue of the arching sky.

"It is the drifting air," explains Fridrik Halldersson, he who has been in the Northern seas. "As the wind buffets the air, it looks blue against the white of the snow. 'Tis the air that makes the dancing shadows."

But Urda shakes her head, and points with her dried finger, and those who stand beside her see figures moving, and airy shapes, and contortions of strange things, such as are seen in a beryl stone.

"But Urda Bjarnason," says Ingeborg Christianson, the pert young wife with the blue-eyed twins, "why is it we see these things only when we stand beside you and you help us to the sight?"

"Because," says the mother, with a steel-blue flash of her old eyes, "having eyes ye will not see!" Then the men laugh. They like to hear Ingeborg worsted. For did she not jilt two men from Gardar, and one from Mountain, and another from Winnipeg?

Not even Ingeborg can deny that Mother Urda tells true things.

"To-day," says Urda, standing by the little window and watching the dance of the shadows, "a child breathed thrice on a farm at the West, and then it died."

The next week at the church gathering, when all the sledges stopped at the house of Urda's granddaughter, they said it was so — that John Christianson's wife Margaret never heard the voice of her son, but that he breathed thrice in his nurse's arms and died.

"Three sledges run over the snow toward Milton," says Urda; "all are laden with wheat, and in one is a stranger. He has with him a strange engine, but its purpose I do not know."

Six hours later the drivers of three empty sledges stop at the house.

"We have been to Milton with wheat," they say, "and Christian Johnson here, carried a photographer from St. Paul."

Now it stands to reason that the farmers like to amuse themselves through the silent and white winters. And they prefer above all things to talk or to listen, as has been the fashion of their race for a thousand years. Among all the story-tellers there is none like Urda, for she is the daughter and the granddaughter and the great-granddaughter of story-tellers. It is given to her to talk, as it is given to John Thorlaksson to sing — he who sings so as his sledge flies over the snow at night, that the people come out in the bitter air from their doors to listen, and the dogs put up their noses and howl, not liking music.

In the little cabin of Peter Christianson, the husband of Urda's granddaughter, it sometimes happens that twenty men will gather about the stove. They hang their bear-skin coats on the wall, put their fur gauntlets underneath the stove, where they will keep warm, and then stretch their stout, felt-covered legs to the wood fire. The room is fetid; the coffee steams eternally on the stove; and from her chair in the warmest corner Urda speaks out to the listening men, who shake their heads with joy as they hear the pure old Icelandic flow in sweet rhythm from between her lips. Among the many, many tales she tells is that of the dead weaver, and she tells it in the simplest language in all the world — language so simple that even great scholars could find no simpler, and the children crawling on the floor can understand.

"Jon and Loa lived with their father and mother far to the north of the Island of Fire, and when the children looked from their windows they saw only wild scaurs and jagged lava rocks, and a distant, deep gleam of the sea. They caught the shine of the sea through an eye-shaped opening in the rocks, and all the long night of winter it gleamed up at them, like the eye of a dead witch. But when it sparkled and began to laugh, the children danced about the hut and sang, for they knew the bright summer time was at hand. Then their father fished, and their mother was gay. But it is true that even in the winter and the darkness they were happy, for they made fishing nets and baskets and cloth together, — Jon and Loa and their father and mother, — and the children were taught to read in the books, and were told the sagas, and given instruction in the part singing.

"They did not know there was such a thing as sorrow in the world, for no one had ever mentioned it to them. But one day their mother died. Then they had to learn how to keep the fire on the hearth, and to smoke the fish, and make the black coffee. And also they had to learn how to live when there is sorrow at the heart.

"They wept together at night for lack of their mother's kisses, and in the morning they were loath to rise because they could not see her face. The dead cold eye of the sea watching them from among the lava rocks made them afraid, so they hung a shawl over the window to keep it out. And the house, try as they would, did not look clean and cheerful as it had used to do when their mother sang and worked about it.

"One day, when a mist rested over the eye of the sea, like that which one beholds on the eyes of the blind, a greater sorrow came to them, for a stepmother crossed the threshold. She looked at Jon and Loa, and made complaint to their father that they were still very small and not likely to be of much use. After that they had to rise earlier than ever, and to work as only those who have their growth should work, till their hearts cracked for weariness and shame. They had not much to eat, for their stepmother said she would trust to the gratitude of no other woman's child, and that she believed in laying up against old age. So she put the few coins that came to the house in a strong box, and bought little food. Neither did she buy the children clothes, though those which their dear mother had made for them were so worn that the warp stood apart from the woof, and there were holes at the elbows and little warmth to be found in them anywhere.

"Moreover, the quilts on their beds were too short for their growing length, so that at night either their purple feet or their thin shoulders were uncovered, and they wept for the cold, and in the morning, when they crept into the larger room to build the fire, they were so stiff they could not stand straight, and there was pain at their joints.

"The wife scolded all the time, and her brow was like a storm sweeping down from the Northwest. There was no peace to be had in the house. The children might not repeat to each other the sagas their mother had taught them, nor try their part singing, nor make little doll cradles of rushes. Always they had to work, always they were scolded, always their clothes grew thinner.

"'Stepmother,' cried Loa one day, — she whom her mother had called the little bird, — 'we are a-cold because of our rags. Our mother would have woven blue cloth for us and made it into garments.'

"'Your mother is where she will weave no cloth!' said the stepmother, and she laughed many times.

"All in the cold and still of that night, the step-mother wakened, and she knew not why. She sat up in her bed, and knew not why. She knew not why, and she looked into the room, and there, by the light of a burning fish's tail — 'twas such a light the folk used in those days — was a woman, weaving. She had no loom, and shuttle she had none. All with her hands she wove a wondrous cloth. Stooping and bending, rising and swaying with motions beautiful as those the Northern Lights make in a midwinter sky, she wove a cloth. The warp was blue and mysti-cal to see, the woof was white, and shone with its whiteness, so that of all the webs the stepmother had ever seen, she had seen none like to this.

"Yet the sight delighted her not, for beyond the drifting web, and beyond the weaver she saw the room and furniture — aye, saw them through the body of the weaver and the drifting of the cloth. Then she knew — as the haunted are made to know — that 'twas the mother of the children come to show her she could still weave cloth. The heart of the stepmother was cold as ice, yet she could not move to waken her husband at her side, for her hands were as fixed as if they were crossed on her dead breast. The voice in her was silent, and her tongue stood to the roof of her mouth.

"After a time the wraith of the dead mother moved toward her — the wraith of the weaver moved her way — and round and about her body was wound the shining cloth. Wherever it touched the body of the stepmother, it was as hateful to her as the touch of a monster out of sea-slime, so that her flesh crept away from it, and her senses swooned.

"In the early morning she awoke to the voices of the children, whispering in the inner room as they dressed with half-frozen fingers. Still about her was the hateful, beautiful web, filling her soul with loathing and with fear. She thought she saw the task set for her, and when the children crept in to light the fire — very purple and thin were their little bodies, and the rags hung from them — she arose and held out the shining cloth, and cried:

"'Here is the web your mother wove for you. I will make it into garments!' But even as she spoke the cloth faded and fell into nothingness, and the children cried:

"'Stepmother, you have the fever!'

"And then:

"'Stepmother, what makes the strange light in the room?'

"That day the stepmother was too weak to rise from her bed, and the children thought she must be going to die, for she did not scold as they cleared the house and braided their baskets, and she did not frown at them, but looked at them with wistful eyes.

"By fall of night she was as weary as if she had wept all the day, and so she slept. But again she was awakened and knew not why. And again she sat up in her bed and knew not why. And again, not knowing why, she looked and saw a woman weaving cloth. All that had happened the night before happened this night. Then, when the morning came, and the children crept in shivering from their beds, she arose and dressed herself, and from her strong box she took coins, and bade her husband go with her to the town.

"So that night a web of cloth, woven by one of the best weavers in all Iceland, was in the house; and on the beds of the children were blankets of lamb's wool, soft to the touch and fair to the eye. After that the children slept warm and were at peace; for now, when they told the sagas their mother had taught them, or tried their part songs as they sat together on their bench, the stepmother was silent. For she feared to chide, lest she should wake at night, not knowing why, and see the mother's wraith."

A GRAMMATICAL GHOST

THERE was only one possible objection to the drawing-room, and that was the occasional presence of Miss Carew; and only one possible objection to Miss Carew. And that was, that she was dead.

She had been dead twenty years, as a matter of fact and record, and to the last of her life sacredly preserved the treasures and traditions of her family, a family bound up — as it is quite unnecessary to explain to any one in good society — with all that is most venerable and heroic in the history of the Republic. Miss Carew never relaxed the proverbial hospitality of her house, even when she remained its sole representative. She continued to preside at her table with dignity and state, and to set an example of excessive modesty and gentle decorum to a generation of restless young women.

It is not likely that having lived a life of such irreproachable gentility as this, Miss Carew would have the bad taste to die in any way not pleasant to mention in fastidious society. She could be trusted to the last, not to outrage those friends who quoted her as an exemplar of propriety. She died very unobtrusively of an affection of the heart, one June morning, while trimming her rose trellis, and her lavender-colored print was not even rumpled when she fell, nor were more than the tips of her little bronze slippers visible.

"Isn't it dreadful," said the Philadelphians, "that the property should go to a very, very distant cousin in Iowa or somewhere else on the frontier, about whom nobody knows anything at all?"

The Carew treasures were packed in boxes and sent away into the Iowa wilderness; the Carew traditions were preserved by the Historical Society; the Carew property, standing in one of the most umbrageous and aristocratic suburbs of Philadelphia, was rented to all manner of folk — anybody who had money enough to pay the rental — and society entered its doors no more.

But at last, after twenty years, and when all save the oldest Philadelphians had forgotten Miss Lydia Carew, the very, very distant cousin appeared. He was quite in the prime of life, and so agreeable and unassuming that nothing could be urged against him save his patronymic, which, being Boggs, did not commend itself to the euphemists. With him were two maiden sisters, ladies of excellent taste and manners, who restored the Carew china to its ancient cabinets, and replaced the Carew pictures upon the walls, with additions not out of keeping with the elegance of these heirlooms. Society, with a magnanimity almost dramatic, overlooked the name of Boggs — and called.

All was well. At least, to an outsider all seemed to be well. But, in truth, there was a certain distress in the old mansion, and in the hearts of the well-behaved Misses Boggs. It came about most unexpectedly. The sisters had been sitting upstairs, looking out at the beautiful grounds of the old place, and marvelling at the violets, which lifted their heads from every possible cranny about the house, and talking over the cordiality which they had been receiving by those upon whom they had no claim, and they were filled with amiable satisfaction. Life looked attractive. They had often been grateful to Miss Lydia Carew for leaving their brother her fortune. Now they felt even more grateful to her. She had left them a Social Position — one, which even after twenty years of desuetude, was fit for use.

They descended the stairs together, with arms clasped about each other's waists, and as they did so presented a placid and pleasing sight. They entered their drawing-room with the intention of brewing a cup of tea, and drinking it in calm sociability in the twilight. But as they entered the room they became aware of the presence of a lady, who was already seated at their tea-table, regarding their old Wedgewood with the air of a connoisseur.

There were a number of peculiarities about this intruder. To begin with, she was hatless, quite as if she were a habitué; of the house, and was costumed in a prim lilac-colored lawn of the style of two decades past. But a greater peculiarity was the resemblance this lady bore to a faded daguerrotype. If looked at one way, she was perfectly discernible; if looked at another, she went out in a sort of blur. Notwithstanding this comparative invisibility, she exhaled a delicate perfume of sweet lavender, very pleasing to the nostrils of the Misses Boggs, who stood looking at her in gentle and unprotesting surprise.

"I beg your pardon," began Miss Prudence, the younger of the Misses Boggs, "but — "

But at this moment the Daguerrotype became a

blur, and Miss Prudence found herself addressing space. The Misses Boggs were irritated. They had never encountered any mysteries in Iowa. They began an impatient search behind doors and portières, and even under sofas, though it was quite absurd to suppose that a lady recognizing the merits of the Carew Wedgewood would so far forget herself as to crawl under a sofa.

When they had given up all hope of discovering the intruder, they saw her standing at the far end of the drawing-room critically examining a water-color marine. The elder Miss Boggs started toward her with stern decision, but the little Daguerrotype turned with a shadowy smile, became a blur and an imperceptibility.

Miss Boggs looked at Miss Prudence Boggs.

"If there were ghosts," she said, "this would be one."

"If there were ghosts," said Miss Prudence Boggs, "this would be the ghost of Lydia Carew."

The twilight was settling into blackness, and Miss Boggs nervously lit the gas while Miss Prudence ran for other tea-cups, preferring, for reasons superfluous to mention, not to drink out of the Carew china that evening.

The next day, on taking up her embroidery frame, Miss Boggs found a number of oldfashioned cross-stitches added to her Kensington. Prudence, she knew, would never have degraded herself by taking a cross-stitch, and the parlor-maid was above taking such a liberty. Miss Boggs mentioned the incident that night at a dinner given by an ancient friend of the Carews.

"Oh, that's the work of Lydia Carew, without a doubt!" cried the hostess. "She visits every new family that moves to the house, but she never remains more than a week or two with any one."

"It must be that she disapproves of them," suggested Miss Boggs.

"I think that's it," said the hostess. "She doesn't like their china, or their fiction."

"I hope she'll disapprove of us," added Miss Prudence.

The hostess belonged to a very old Philadelphian family, and she shook her head.

"I should say it was a compliment for even the ghost of Miss Lydia Carew to approve of one," she said severely.

The next morning, when the sisters entered their drawing-room there were numerous evidences of an occupant during their absence. The sofa pillows had been rearranged so that the effect of their grouping was less bizarre than that favored by the Western women; a horrid little Buddhist idol with its eyes fixed on its abdomen, had been chastely hidden behind a Dresden shepherdess, as unfit for the scrutiny of polite eyes; and on the table where Miss Prudence did work in water colors, after the fashion of the impressionists, lay a prim and impossible composition representing a moss-rose and a number of heartsease, colored with that caution which modest spinster artists instinctively exercise.

"Oh, there's no doubt it's the work of Miss Lydia Carew," said Miss Prudence, contemptuously. "There's no mistaking the drawing of that rigid little rose. Don't you remember those wreaths and bouquets framed, among the pictures we got when the Carew pictures were sent to us? I gave some of them to an orphan asylum and burned up the rest."

"Hush!" cried Miss Boggs, involuntarily. "If she heard you, it would hurt her feelings terribly. Of course, I mean — " and she blushed. "It might hurt her feelings — but how perfectly ridiculous! It's impossible!"

Miss Prudence held up the sketch of the moss-rose.

"THAT may be impossible in an artistic sense, but it is a palpable thing."

"Bosh!" cried Miss Boggs.

"But," protested Miss Prudence, "how do you explain it?"

"I don't," said Miss Boggs, and left the room.

That evening the sisters made a point of being in the drawing-room before the dusk came on, and of lighting the gas at the first hint of twilight. They didn't believe in Miss Lydia Carew — but still they meant to be beforehand with her. They talked with unwonted vivacity and in a louder tone than was their custom. But as they drank their tea even their utmost verbosity could not make them oblivious to the fact that the perfume of sweet lavender was stealing insidiously through the room. They tacitly refused to recognize this odor and all that it indicated, when suddenly, with a sharp crash, one of the old Carew tea-cups fell from the tea-table to the floor and was broken. The disaster was followed by what sounded like a sigh of pain and dismay.

"I didn't suppose Miss Lydia Carew would ever be as awkward as that," cried the younger Miss Boggs, petulantly.

"Prudence," said her sister with a stern accent, "please try not to be a fool. You brushed the cup off with the sleeve of your dress."

"Your theory wouldn't be so bad," said Miss Prudence, half laughing and half crying, "if there were any sleeves to my dress, but, as you see, there aren't," and then Miss Prudence had something as near hysterics as a healthy young woman from the West can have.

"I wouldn't think such a perfect lady as Lydia Carew," she ejaculated between her sobs, "would make herself so disagreeable! You may talk about good-breeding all you please, but I call such intrusion exceedingly bad taste. I have a horrible idea that she likes us and means to stay with us. She left those other people because she did not approve of their habits or their grammar. It would be just our luck to please her."

"Well, I like your egotism," said Miss Boggs.

However, the view Miss Prudence took of the case appeared to be the right one. Time went by and Miss Lydia Carew still remained. When the ladies entered their drawing-room they would see the little lady-like Daguerrotype revolving itself into a blur before one of the family portraits. Or they noticed that the yellow sofa cushion, toward which she appeared to feel a peculiar antipathy, had been dropped behind the sofa upon the floor, or that one of Jane Austen's novels, which none of the family ever read, had been removed from the book shelves and left open upon the table.

"I cannot become reconciled to it," complained Miss Boggs to Miss Prudence. "I wish we had remained in Iowa where we belong. Of course I don't believe in the thing! No sensible person would. But still I cannot become reconciled."

But their liberation was to come, and in a most unexpected manner.

A relative by marriage visited them from the West. He was a friendly man and had much to say, so he talked all through dinner, and afterward followed the ladies to the drawing-room to finish his gossip. The gas in the room was turned very low, and as they entered Miss Prudence caught sight of Miss Carew, in company attire, sitting in upright propriety in a stiff-backed chair at the extremity of the apartment.

Miss Prudence had a sudden idea.

"We will not turn up the gas," she said, with an emphasis intended to convey private information to her sister. "It will be more agreeable to sit here and talk in this soft light."

Neither her brother nor the man from the West

made any objection. Miss Boggs and Miss Prudence, clasping each other's hands, divided their attention between their corporeal and their incorporeal guests. Miss Boggs was confident that her sister had an idea, and was willing to await its development. As the guest from Iowa spoke, Miss Carew bent a politely attentive ear to what he said.

"Ever since Richards took sick that time," he said briskly, "it seemed like he shed all responsibility." (The Misses Boggs saw the Daguerrotype put up her shadowy head with a movement of doubt and apprehension.) "The fact of the matter was, Richards didn't seem to scarcely get on the way he might have been expected to." (At this conscienceless split to the infinitive and misplacing of the preposition, Miss Carew arose trembling perceptibly.) "I saw it wasn't no use for him to count on a quick recovery — "

The Misses Boggs lost the rest of the sentence, for at the utterance of the double negative Miss Lydia Carew had flashed out, not in a blur, but with mortal haste, as when life goes out at a pistol shot!

The man from the West wondered why Miss Prudence should have cried at so pathetic a part of his story:

"Thank Goodness!"

And their brother was amazed to see Miss Boggs kiss Miss Prudence with passion and energy.

It was the end. Miss Carew returned no more.